LILY RENÉE,
Escape Artist

From Holocaust Survivor to Comic Book Pioneer

TRINA ROBBINS

Illustrated by
ANNE TIMMONS and MO OH

GRAPHIC UNIVERSE™ · MINNEAPOLIS · NEW YORK

Story by
Trina Robbins

Pencils by
Anne Timmons

Inks by
mo oh

Lettering by
Felix Ruiz and Cayetano Garza Jr.

Coloring by
Studio C10

Text copyright © 2011 by Trina Robbins
Illustrations copyright © 2011 by Lerner Publishing Group, Inc.

Graphic Universe™ is a trademark of Lerner Publishing Group, Inc.

Graphic Universe™
A division of Lerner Publishing Group, Inc.
241 First Avenue North
Minneapolis, MN 55401 U.S.A.

Website address: www.lernerbooks.com

Photographs on pp. 4, 79, 94, and 95 are courtesy of Lily Renée Phillips. The comic book art photographed on pp. 92 and 93 are from the collection of the author.

Main body text set in CC Dave Gibbons Lower.
Typeface provided by Comicraft/Active Images.

Library of Congress Cataloging-in-Publication Data

Robbins, Trina.
   Lily Renée, escape artist : from Holocaust survivor to comic book pioneer / by Trina Robbins ; illustrated by Anne Timmons and mo oh.
      p.   cm.
   ISBN: 978-0-7613-6010-0 (lib. bdg. : alk. paper)
   1. Renée, Lily — Biography — Juvenile literature. 2. Jewish children in the Holocaust — Germany — Biography — Juvenile literature. 3. Holocaust, Jewish (1939-1945) — Germany — Biography — Juvenile literature. 4. Germany — Ethnic relations — Juvenile literature. I. Timmons, Anne. II. Oh, Margaret. III. Title.
DS134.42.R46 R63 2011
940.53'18092—dc22
   [B]   2011001084

Manufactured in the United States of America
2 – DP – 2/1/12

CHAPTER ONE: *Vienna, 1938*

Growing up in Vienna, the capitol of Austria, in the 1930s, Lily Renée Wilheim experienced the best of everything.

Vienna was a gracious and cultured city, with museums, a famous opera, and beautiful old buildings.

Lily's family was well-off. Her father managed the Holland America line, a big steamship company that ran transatlantic travel and cargo shipments, and provided elegant vacation cruises.

Her parents took Lily to the ballet, and she visited the opera twice a year with her school.

Lily attended dancing classes and art school. She was a talented artist, and while she was still very young, her art was exhibited at a gallery.

One day, it all changed...

On March 12, 1938, Hitler's Nazi army invaded Austria.

Long before the Nazis came to power, Austria had wanted to form a union with *Germany* and bring all German peoples together into one country. The word for this union was ***Anschluss.***

They longed to recapture past glory. Also, Hitler had been born in Austria, and many Austrians belonged to the Nazi Party.

Wildly enthusiastic crowds cheered the Nazis as they marched into the capital city of Vienna.

But not everyone was enthusiastic.

Mama, Papa, I'm scared.

So are we, *liebling.*

Lily and her parents were Jewish. They knew how fiercely the Nazis hated the Jews.

Almost immediately, the Nazis began to persecute the Austrian Jews.

On April 10, an election was held. 99% of the votes were in favor of Austria becoming part of Germany. Most people were afraid to vote no, in case their votes should be made public. Jews were not allowed to vote.

The Nazis confiscated Jewish property.

Nazi headquarters needs a radio. We're taking this one.

But, Mama, that's our only radio.

Shh.

The Nazis forced all Jewish merchants to mark their stores. Then the Nazis stood outside the stores, urging people not to shop there.

JUDE

Nazis made all the Jews in Austria move to Vienna. Viennese Jews with large houses or apartments had to share them with the displaced Jews.

You'll have to share your apartment with these people. You have plenty of room.

≿Sigh≾

I guess we'll fit them in somehow.

Lily, Mr. and Mrs. Popper need to get these papers stamped. The lines are so long, and they both have arthritis. Will you get their papers stamped for them?

Of course, Mama.

Thank you, little one.

Ugh, this will take hours.

Everyone's so quiet.

They're afraid to speak.

EVERYBODY OUT!

In Berlin, a seventeen-year-old Jewish boy named Herschel Grynzpan, protesting the brutal treatment of his family by the Nazis, had shot and killed a German diplomat.

The Nazis retaliated by starting riots in Berlin and Vienna, with mobs led by the *Gestapo* disguised as citizens.

So this time they really did burn the synagogue.

It's not safe anymore. We have to leave Austria.

Because of the broken glass covering the sidewalks and streets, this night was named Kristallnacht, or *The Night of Broken Glass.*

CHAPTER TWO: *Kindertransport, 1939*

CHAPTER THREE: *England*

Every day, on his way back from work, Molly's father picked up Molly at school.

We're back, Mum! When's tea? I'm hungry!

Not as hungry as I am.

Liebling, we were so happy to hear from you! Mama is knitting a sweater for you to wear on those rainy English summer days. Maybe we'll see you so soon that we can bring the sweater instead of sending it! Meanwhile, please write often.

Another slice of toast, Lily? You'll get fat if you keep eating like that!

Oh, Mama, Papa! I miss you so much! But I can't tell you how unhappy I am.

Mama, Papa, I'm miserable here! Mrs. Kealy hates me because I can't do her housework, so she's starving me. I'm living on high tea.

Dearest Mama and Papa, I know I will love the sweater, but I don't need it right now. The weather here is very pleasant. By the time you get here, it will be cooler, and I will be happy to have the sweater! My English is getting better, and I no longer have trouble understanding what people are saying. When you see me, you will think I am an English girl...

34

On September 3, 1939, the prime minister of England, Neville Chamberlain, made an announcement over the radio to the British people.

I am speaking to you from the cabinet room at 10 Downing Street…

…This country is at war with Germany…

That's it, then. War.

You can imagine what a bitter blow it is to me that all my long struggle to win peace has failed…

Oh, Lily! Your parents!

…I know that you will all play your part with calmness and courage.

Now I can never get them out of the country!

Hmmph. Guess we're stuck with you, Lily.

That night, while everyone slept, Lily packed up and left.

Now what?
My cousin Greta lives in London, but I hardly know her. And anyway, how can she help me? She's just a housemaid, living in a tiny room.

Not a penny for the bus.

No matter. I'll walk to Leeds.

CHAPTER FOUR: *Leeds*

CHAPTER FIVE: *The Blitz*

45

After the all-clear siren sounded, they cautiously emerged from the shelters.

We'll never surrender!

Thank goodness the hospital wasn't hit.

If Hitler thinks he'll get us down, he's wrong.

The Blitz finally ended in May 1941. The records show that by then, 18,629 men, 16,201 women, and 5,028 children had been killed by the Nazi bombs.

Lily spent her days working hard, but at night she worried...about home, about being called an enemy alien.

A letter for you, Lily.

For me? Who...?

It's from the Jewish Refugee Agency at Bloomsbury House!

Bloomsbury House, in London, was the central office for Jewish refugees. They found homes for the Kindertransport children and they reunited families that had been split apart by the war.

My parents are safe in America! They've sent for me! They're putting me on a ship that leaves in two days!

That's wonderful, Lily! I'm so happy for you!

CHAPTER SIX: *"Enemy Alien"*

CHAPTER EIGHT: *Getting By in New York*

Lily started out erasing the pencil lines on other people's pages and drawing backgrounds.

Then they gave her a feature to draw, a supernatural horror series called *Werewolf Hunter.*

Next, they gave her a story called Jane Martin about a woman pilot who fought the Nazis.

Lily Renée continued to live in New York. She married and raised a family. After she stopped drawing comics in 1949, she created textile designs and designed jewelry. She wrote and illustrated children's books and wrote five plays.

Her two children and four grandchildren grew up proud that their grandmother was a comic book artist.

Señorita Rio was a fantasy for me. She got clothes that I couldn't have, she had a leopard coat, and she wore high-end shoes and had grand adventures and was very daring and beautiful and glamorous.

And through Señorita Rio, Lily Renée was able to do what she couldn't do on her own...

Beat the Nazis.

More about

LILY'S STORY

GLOSSARY, *German to English*

Anschluss: a German term meaning "link up." This word was used to describe unifying Germany and Austria in 1938, to bring all German peoples together into one country.

Blitz: short for *Blitzkrieg*, which translates as "Lightning War." It was so named because the surprise attacks were lightning fast but also because the bombs were like deadly lightning raining down from the sky. Germany started daily air attacks on major cities in England in September 1940. The Blitz finally ended in May 1941.

Kindertransport: Children's Transport. Kindertransport lasted from December 1, 1938, to September 1, 1939, when England went to war against Germany. About 10,000 children escaped from the Nazis this way.

Kristallnacht: Crystal Night, also called the Night of Broken Glass, so named for the shards of broken glass scattered on the sidewalks after the shop windows of Jewish merchants had been smashed on the night of November 9–10, 1938.

liebling: loved one, dearest. This is what Lily's parents called her.

Nazi: a member of the Nationalist Socialist German Workers' Party, the political party that ruled Germany from 1933–1945. The Nazi Party spread hatred and violence against ethnic minorities, the physically and mentally disabled, members of other political parties, and Jews, among others. While they were in power, many people became members of the Nazi Party out of fear.

In the story, the two different types of word balloons show whether people are speaking (or writing or thinking) in German or in English.

THE CONCENTRATION CAMPS

The first concentration camps were built in Germany in 1933 after the Nazis took control of the country. In the beginning they contained opponents of the new government, political prisoners, and other people that Hitler considered "enemies of the state": Communists, Socialists, Jehovah's Witnesses, homosexuals, and Roma (the nomadic people sometimes referred to as Gypsies). They were called concentration camps because all the prisoners were physically concentrated in one place.

After the Nazis marched into Austria in 1938, they started sending German and Austrian Jews to camps called Dachau, Buchenwald, and Sachsenhausen, all located in Germany. When Hitler invaded Poland in 1939, the Nazis opened labor camps there, where thousands of Polish prisoners died from exhaustion, starvation, and exposure. Soon the Nazis were arresting Jews, Polish people, mentally and physically disabled people, and other "undesirables" from *all* the countries they conquered, and building more camps to confine them. In 1941, the Nazis invaded the Soviet Union and established prisoner of war camps there, for captured Soviet soldiers. Eventually, about 20,000 camps and detention centers were built.

The prisoners were taken to the camps in filthy, cramped trains meant for cattle, with no food or water sometimes for days. Once they arrived at the camps, those who were young and healthy were turned into slave laborers. They were starved and overworked until many died from exhaustion, malnutrition, or exposure. The very young and the very old and all others who couldn't work were immediately sent to their deaths.

No matter what the camps were called, whether they were labor camps or prisoner of war camps, the end result was almost always death for the inmates. But certain camps made no pretense of what they were. Places such as Auschwitz–Birkenau were simply extermination camps. The purpose of the extermination camps was to kill as many prisoners—usually Jews—as they could, as quickly as possible.

For this purpose, the Nazis built gas chambers, rooms filled with poison gas. Auschwitz–Birkenau had four gas chambers, and during the height of the war, up to 6,000 people were murdered in the chambers every day.

Hitler's aim was to destroy all the Jews in the world. By the time the concentration camps were liberated in 1945, he had succeeded in murdering over three million Jews, along with many of his other "undesirables."

It is a miracle that anyone at all survived these hideous places of mass torture, starvation, and death.

THE INTERNMENT CAMPS

In 1939, England went to war with Germany and suddenly all refugees from Nazi-occupied countries were considered possible spies or saboteurs. Refugees from the ages of 16 to 70 were classified as "enemy aliens" and shipped off to internment camps on the Isle of Man and also to camps in Canada and Australia.

These camps were nothing like the Nazi concentration camps, but they weren't happy places, either. They certainly were nothing like summer camps! In many cases, accommodations were very basic and primitive. Husbands and wives were split apart, as men and women were sent to separate camps, although later, England opened a camp for families. On the other hand, the Isle of Man had been a resort island where British families went for their summer vacations. So the people who were sent there (called *internees*) were housed in holiday cottages.

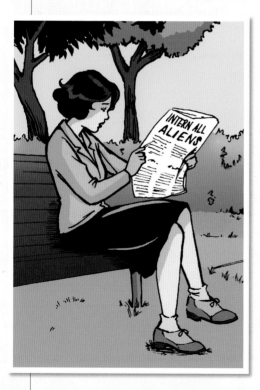

Because they were not allowed to have newspapers, some of the internees wrote and printed their own camp newspapers. Others formed schools and theaters. Many of the young men joined the British armed forces. They bravely fought the Nazis.

In 1941, when the United States entered the war, the "enemy aliens" were reclassified as "friendly aliens." The camps were closed, but not before two terrible incidents.

In June 1940, the ship *Andorra Star* was transporting refugees from England to an internment camp in Canada when she was torpedoed and sank. All 743 internees, crew, and guards perished.

In July 1940, the ship *Dunera* left Liverpool with 2,542 "enemy aliens," most of whom were Jewish refugees, on board. They were bound for an internment camp in Australia. The *Dunera* was only meant to carry 1,500 people, including crew, so conditions were horribly overcrowded. On top of that, the British guards mistreated the internees, taking away their possessions and beating and insulting them. Moreover, the passengers knew that during the 57-day voyage to Australia, the *Dunera* was under constant risk of being torpedoed by the Nazis like the *Andorra Star* had been.

When the *Dunera* docked in Sydney, Australia, the first person to go on board was a medical army officer named Alan Frost. He took one look at the terrible conditions and filed a report that led to the court-martial (a trial for a soldier in a military court) of the army officer in charge.

AFTERNOON TEA, HIGH TEA, DINNER? *I Give Up!*

Until recently, meals in England had different names and were eaten at different times than meals in Europe or the United States. Dinner, the main meal that most Americans eat in the evening, was usually eaten in England sometime between noon and 1:30 P.M. Then, in the evening, when most Americans were settling down to their heavy meal, the British sat down to high tea.

High tea was a light meal, more like lunch in the United States. But it featured food that might seem rather strange, if not downright unappetizing, to other people's tastes. Traditionally, high tea included something sweet such as scones, cakes, or sweet breads. Along with that would be pickles, cold meats, or poached eggs on toast. And, of course, tea. The tea came from a teapot, never from tea bags in a cup.

During the war, high teas were not as sumptuous as they had been. Fresh meat and eggs were scarce, so British housewives started adding a lot of canned foods to the tea table: canned spaghetti, canned kippers (a small salted or pickled fish), and canned beans on toast. Dessert would likely be canned pears served with canned milk. And, of course, tea from a teapot.

To make things even more confusing, there was another kind of tea, called afternoon tea. This was a centuries-old tradition usually indulged in by wealthy people. It consisted of dainty sandwiches—a favorite was thinly sliced cucumber on white buttered bread with the crusts cut off—along with pastries and scones, served with jams and a thick cream. Tea was poured, usually by servants, from silver teapots into delicate china teacups.

It's easy to see why Lily was confused!

HOW CAN ANYTHING BE WORTH
Less Than a Penny?

If dinner, high tea, and afternoon tea are confusing, British money was even more confusing. There were farthings, ha'pennies, thrup-pennies, groats, shillings, pounds, guineas, and sovereigns.

And the money had nicknames! A shilling was called a bob, a two-shilling coin was called a florin, and a pound was called a quid. A guinea was worth one pound and one shilling, and a sovereign was a gold coin worth one pound. A groat was worth four pence (pennies), thruppence meant a three-penny coin, and ha'penny was short for "half a penny." There was even a coin smaller than a ha'penny: one-quarter of a penny, called a farthing!

It may seem ridiculous now that anyone would need one-fourth of a penny. But prices were much lower in wartime England. In 1939, a pound of butter cost 7½ pence, and a pound of margarine was 2½ pence. You could buy a pound of apples for 1½ pence and a pound of cookies for 5 pence.

It wasn't until 1971 that this confusing system was simplified into just pounds and pence, but you would still see shillings around for years after that. Ever since 1999, the euro has been used as a single currency in more and more of Europe, making it possible to use the same money as you travel from country to country. But the British have opted to keep using the pound.

Just as the U.S. dollar is worth 100 pennies, the English pound is worth 100 pence. But even today, a pound is still nicknamed a quid!

CHAMBERLAIN *vs.* CHURCHILL

It was Prime Minister Neville Chamberlain, not the more famous Winston Churchill, who declared war against the Nazis in September 1939.

Neville Chamberlain became prime minister in 1937. He had strong experience in government, but many people say he had poor judgment. He was soft and patient in dealing with Germany when Hitler and the Nazi Party came to power. Chamberlain hoped his approach would prevent the outbreak of a major war, but in the end, his weak peace treaties failed to stop World War II.

In poor health, Chamberlain resigned in May 1940. This made way for Winston Churchill to become prime minister. Winston Churchill is widely considered to be one of the greatest political leaders of the twentieth century. Many quotes from his speeches are often repeated today.

One of Churchill's most famous quotes, after a devastating loss to the Nazis, was his promise that "we shall fight on the beaches, we shall fight on the landing grounds, we shall fight in the fields and in the streets, we shall fight in the hills. We shall never surrender." Another famous quote was when he praised all the soldiers who fought in the war, saying that never "was so much owed by so many to so few."

Churchill presided over Great Britain for six years, leading the British people to victory in 1945. He is often seen in photographs holding up one hand in a "V for Victory" sign.

History does not paint a kind picture of Prime Minister Chamberlain. His soft policies toward the Nazis, known as appeasement, are still held up today as an example and a warning for current political leaders of what not to do. Churchill himself compared appeasement to being like someone who "feeds a crocodile—hoping it will eat him last."

Queen WILHELMINA

Queen Wilhelmina was queen of the Netherlands (Holland) from 1890 to 1948. This makes her one of the longest-reigning monarchs in European history. She occupied the throne during both World War I and II, and reigned over her country through many challenges. Known as an intelligent and strong woman, Queen Wilhelmina became a great inspiration to the Dutch (the people of the Netherlands) during their difficult struggle when the Nazis occupied their country from 1940 to 1945.

When she was offered a safe refuge in England during the war by King George VI, she reluctantly accepted. She continued to lead her country from afar. Her radio broadcasts to millions of her fellow citizens were a boost to their morale.

The Dutch people and Queen Wilhelmina regained their freedom from the Nazis in March 1945.

THE *Holland America* LINE

Lily's father, Rudolph Wilheim, managed the Austrian branch of the Holland America Line, a historic and highly respected steamship company. Its first ship, the *Rotterdam*, sailed from Holland to New York in 1873.

The ship that took Lily to New York was the *Rotterdam IV*. It had been built in 1908, and Lily may have been a passenger on its last voyage, because it was sold for scrap in 1940. But in its heyday, the *Rotterdam IV* was first class throughout. It boasted of "56 suites and rooms with brass bedsteads and private baths, and over 100 single rooms, together with a beautiful Palm Court, Verandah Cafe, Elevator, Social Hall, Library, 3 Smoke Rooms, a glass enclosed Promenade Deck, electronically forced ventilation of hot and cold air, etc."

One of the ship's most attractive features was an immense dining saloon that could seat nearly five hundred people. Passengers dined on French cuisine beneath crystal chandeliers while serenaded by a full orchestra. When Lily and the other Kindertransport kids wandered the old ship, its halls must have been filled with faded glory and the ghostly reminders of a long-past age of carefree elegance.

HORN & HARDART: *The Automat*

Horn & Hardart, better known as the Automat, was a unique chain of restaurants that was popular from the early 1900s through the late 1960s.

In 1888, Joseph Horn and Frank Hardart opened their first restaurant in Philadelphia. The tiny luncheonette was only 11 feet by 17 feet and had no tables, only a counter with fifteen stools, but the delicious coffee they served made it extremely popular.

It wasn't until 1902 that Horn and Hardart opened their first Automat in Philadelphia, followed ten years later by two Automats in New York City. What made these restaurants so unusual was their way of serving food.

Instead of sitting at a table and being waited on, customers went first to glass booths where women cashiers changed their money into nickels. Then customers took their nickels to a wall of small glass windows behind which plates of food sat on little glass shelves. The shelves had sections for cooked food—mac and cheese, meat loaf, and pot pies were some customer favorites—and there were sections for cakes and pies and desserts. Customers placed their nickels into slots next to the dish they chose and turned a little handle. The glass window popped open, and diners helped themselves to their food. Once they closed the window again, the shelf revolved, and *presto!* there sat another plate of food, ready for the next customer's nickels.

By the 1950s, Horn & Hardart had grown so popular that there were 180 Automats in New York and Philadelphia. In Manhattan alone, there were 40 Automats. By the 1960s, those nickels had become quarters, but the Automat remained a place where people could get tasty, cheap food. The very last Automat closed in 1991.

In the 1940s, you could buy a good, filling lunch at the Automat for 5 nickels—25 cents. Another nickel would buy you a cup of coffee. But poor Lily couldn't even spare that much money and had to rely on "free lemonade"!

Jane Martin by Fran Hopper

Toni Gayle by Joyce Valleau

Miss Fury by Tarpé Mills

The Fighting Femmes
OF WARTIME COMIC BOOKS
AND THEIR ARTISTS

Up until World War II, for the most part, women were expected to marry, stay home, and raise a family while their husbands went off to work. But the war changed all that. After the United States entered the war in 1941, many young men left their jobs on farms, in offices, and in factories to join the armed forces and fight the enemy overseas. Who was going to take over the jobs they had left behind? Women! The new image of women was of a determined character called Rosie the Riveter. In posters, Rosie the Riveter is shown rolling up her sleeve and saying, "We can do it!"

Women were driving trucks and buses, working in factories and shipyards making ships and planes...and, yes, they were drawing comics.

Toni Gayle by Joyce Valleau

Señorita Rio by Lily Renée

Brenda Starr by Dale Messick

    The image of women in the pages of comic books changed too. Until the war, women in comic books were usually the girlfriend of the hero. All too often they existed just so that he would have someone to rescue. But during the war, a new kind of woman appeared in comics. Like her real-life sisters, she was strong and determined, but she went one step further. Heroines such as Miss Fury, Black Cat, and the Girl Commandos dressed up in costumes like the male superheroes and fought criminals and Nazis. Sometimes they had patriotic names like Miss America. And sometimes they were plainclothes heroines, such as the beautiful spy Señorita Rio, the flying nurse Jane Martin, "girl detective" Toni Gayle, or "girl reporter" Brenda Starr.

    And every one of the comics heroines listed above was drawn or created by women!

Lily's PHOTO ALBUM

Lily Renée Wilheim at 6 years of age

Lily and her mother

Lily's father, Rudolph Wilheim

13-year-old Lily with her mother and friends

Mr. Katz, who took care of the kids on the *Rotterdam* on their way to America

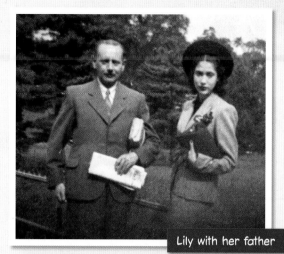

Lily with her father

Lily with her mother on Lily's first day in New York

Lily at work, drawing comics

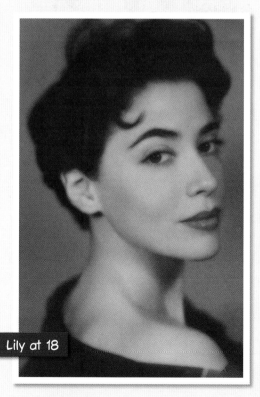

Lily at 18

Lily today, with some pages of her art

Trina Robbins is the Eisner and Harvey Award–nominated author of numerous nonfiction and fiction books and comics for children and adults, including several histories of women cartoonists. A pioneer in comics herself, she took part in the underground comix movement of the 1960s and illustrated the Wonder Woman comic book. Most recently, she authored the Chicagoland Detective Agency graphic novel series. She lives in San Francisco with her partner, comics artist Steve Leialoha.

Anne Timmons was born in Portland, Oregon, and received her BFA from Oregon State University. In addition to her collaboration with Trina Robbins on the Lulu Award–winning GoGirl!, her work includes the Eisner-nominated *Dignifying Science* and *Pigling: A Cinderella Story* for the Graphic Myths and Legends series. She has illustrated and painted covers for children's books and provided interior and cover art for regional and national magazines, including *Wired*, *Portland Review*, and *Comic Book Artist*. Her art also appears in the anthology *9-11: Artists Respond* and is now in the Library of Congress.

mo oh likes to draw. She also likes to read, bake, eat (mostly eat), make plants grow (mainly for eating), and sit in the sun. She graduated from the Center for Cartoon Studies with an MFA in cartooning and works on and off as a sketch/concept artist for a small game company. She lives in Massachusetts.